In Australia's Back of Beyond, he parked at the top of a deep gorge.
Inside a huge cave, blinding words blazed on the rock wall.

T0148382

IN THE NEVER NEVER GOD TOLD ME THIS

By

Noel Stevens

He wanted to shoot himself. He read the refulgent words :
"You can get your rifle...or you can chat with Me."

"I will never leave you – I can't, because I made you."

iUniverse, Inc.
New York   Bloomington

In The Never Never God Told Me This

iUniverse books may be ordered through booksellers or by contacting:

iUniverse
1663 Liberty Drive
Bloomington, IN 47403
www.iuniverse.com
1-800-Authors (1-800-288-4677)

ISBN: 978-1-4401-0574-6 (pbk)
ISBN: 978-1-4401-0575-3 (ebk)

Printed in the United States of America

iUniverse rev. date: 6/23/2009

"I have never said "do" or "don't"...that would take away from you that treasure, your priceless free-will.

This was some of the oldest rocky country on earth, Australia's far north-west, the Back of Beyond.

A flat ledge led me to the bigger of two more caves – about forty feet high and fifteen feet wide. It had a flat floor that went in some fifty feet.

I explored it carefully. It was clean of anything that might bite or sting. Ten years ago, an old aboriginal had told me that thousands and thousands of years ago, this cave had been sacred – it came from the Dreaming Time. For uncounted thousands of years, no animal, no bird, no snake or insect ever went in there, he said.

"Today, hundreds of millions in the West...go uncomforted to the tomb. They cling in despair to their...consciousness which they think death will extinguish.

Heartfelt thanks to Sarah Slover, for your originality.

IN THE NEVER NEVER GOD
TOLD ME THIS

I drove the Land Rover slowly over rocky ground, the wheels jolting. It brushed by chest-high shrubs, but I steered away from the gum trees with their tall, bare, white trunks.

This was some of the oldest rocky country on earth, Australia's far north-west, the Back of Beyond.

I knew that on my left, ochre cliffs fell down to two wide, shallow pools. I knew the green-blue water would be cool, with cascades flowing into them, and water running out at the bottom over the rocks. The Land Rover splashed through a shallow creek on the rock – water for the pools.

I swung around, following the curve of the cliff edge, and ragged, beige rocks rose steeply up on my right to the distant sky. Three hundred yards more and I reached the immense cave – the roof about one hundred and fifty feet high and almost as wide. I drove in about fifteen yards till the front bumper touched the back wall. The sun would never reach the Land Rover in this shallow hangar of rock.

Getting out stiffly, I walked along the narrowing ledge of the cliff top to two caves, and explored them carefully. They were clean and empty. Each could hold three large tents easily.

Walking to the cliff edge, I peered down at the pools. I was too far up. Back at the Land Rover, I packed a big pack, and walked carefully down a natural slope.

The vast block of ragged rock was dark, reddish brown. A flat ledge led me to the bigger of two more caves – about forty feet high and fifteen feet wide. It had a flat floor that went in some fifty feet.

I explored it carefully. It was clean of anything that might bite or sting. Ten years ago, an old aboriginal had told me that thousands and thousands of years ago, this cave had been sacred – it came from the Dreaming Time. For uncounted thousands of years, no animal, no bird, no snake or insect once went in there, he said.

After setting up my five-man, mosquito-netting, floored tent, I pumped up the air mattress, put it inside, and zipped the tent up tight. Then I unloaded the pack.

It was a hard climb up to the Land Rover, where I filled the pack again.

I looked across miles of ancient rocks and scattered green trees and shrubs. A light wind stirred the air.

After our two sons and daughter grew up and married, my wife, and I had spent twenty-five years in the deserts, mountains and rocky country, while I did my work as a geologist. We were never lonely.

Joan poured out love endlessly – when she died, my world

fell in. I found what a loveless world I lived in, what a lonely one. For a year I tried living in Melbourne, but my sons and daughter ignored me. When they saw me, they always asked for money...

My two brothers and three sisters had bitter minds. My brothers had three daughters, and all three needed psychiatric support. Two of my brothers-in-law were alcoholics – everyone said my sisters drove them to it.

Now they were about 2,000 miles away in Melbourne, but their gall, the acridity, their spite was in the air about me.

I felt suicidal.

The loneliness of the vast spaces had been my joy – now I felt solitary, abandoned, fearful in a primeval land. I stared around me.

Taking several deep breaths, I struggled into the shoulder straps, and carried the backpack down. In the cave, I unloaded it, and carried a second air mattress, with a cooking stove and food, to the edge of the top pool.

Stripping, I fell into the cool water, and swam lazily. I floated, then swam to a shallow edge, and lay on rock with the water just covering me.

I went back to my things, put on underpants, and cooked a meal. The breeze soon dried me and as I felt warmed, I went back in and came out wet to eat my lunch.

Afterwards, warding off the panic of my loneliness, I had a nap on the mattress, and dreamt of Joan, my wife.

Back in the cave, I straightened out all my things. I felt more and more suicidal, and thought of the rifle.

The tent was well into the cave, and I had about twenty feet from my tent to the entrance.

My things were on the floor of the cave, and I had just checked my video camera, when a strange paralysis gripped me. I went into a sort of trance.

Suddenly, I saw writing on the cave wall, and a voice told me, "Set up your camera."

I felt powerless, and set up the camera like an automaton.

Then I read the words.

"I am the Lord thy God. You want to use your rifle. Will we chat?"

I sat stunned, unable to speak a word.

Then I croaked, "God? Come down from heaven? Am I hallucinating?"

"You are not hallucinating," appeared on the wall.

"You are God?"

"I am the Holy Spirit, the Eternal Spirit. In the very ancient of days, I came forth from the Godhead, which is ineffable, unchanging and changeless love and joy, perfect awareness. The

Godhead willed me to separate Myself out of Him to enter into time and change, to create this cosmos, and other dimensions."

"Then you are not God?"

On the wall, I read – and photographed – the words, "Incarnated within your earthy body is your eternal Spirit, which always was and always will be. Your Spirit came forth from the Godhead, as did I. We are both of the same substance as our Father."

I realised I had turned the sound on, on my camera, so the machine recorded my voice.

I stuttered, "Why have you appeared to me? I'm not religious."

The words came onto the wall. "This is holy ground. Thirty thousand years ago, I made visitations here to the aborigines."

I mumbled, while my hand, not of its own volition, turned the sound fully up.

"Aborigines cannot read or write."

He answered, the words on the wall. "In heaven spirits have no brains. We share our feelings and images, without words. Words need a brain. Sometimes, I projected aboriginal words into their minds. Do you wish to chat with Me?"

I asked, "If you created the universe, why did you bring so much pain and agony into the earth? Back in the time of the dinosaurs, some of them hunted, and tore others to pieces."

I cried, "The agony! The agony many humans suffer!"

On the wall. "Doctors can stop the pain. If they don't, it's from their sadism."

"Do You feel pain?"

"Did you feel your wife's pain when she was dying?"

"I could imagine it. I went mad. But not directly..."

"I do not feel directly. In heaven, the Godhead is perfect awareness, and He experiences what you do directly.

"Don't think I haven't heard the weeping in your heart. You can take up your rifle. But I am your comfort, am always with you.

"Hear what I say. Heaven and earth may pass away, but your Spirit shall live, as it has already lived, from everlasting to everlasting.

"You can go and get your rifle, or I can chat with you, and you can listen, and you can chat with Me.

"I have come here to you if you want Me here. Afterwards, I can show you things you may care to know, if you will let Me.

"You can chat with Me as with a friend closer to you than you are to yourself. You can chat with Me as One who loves you far more than you love yourself."

I whispered, "I can't find words."

Then I said, "Can You speak to me directly, instead of writing?"

"You will hear My words in your head, and afterwards you will have no record. But My words on the wall will stay on your film. Afterwards, you will set up your word processor, and replay the film, looking in your viewfinder. As you replay, you will write down every word, from your sound track, and from your film.

"But what are words? Spirits say everything with feelings and images. Words are like paper money. You give a piece of coloured paper and receive a loaf of bread. The bread is real – the paper is indigestible. It is the importance you give to the paper money – in some countries, millions devote their lives to seize more and more of this coloured paper.

"Words are like that. It is the importance you give to them, your human brains. Words are noises that substitute for your real thoughts and feelings.

"They are symbols that you use to make yourself understood. They are never real, any more than a film of lions in Africa is real. For the reality, you must travel to Africa, watch the lions with your own eyes, smell them, hear them..."

"My family seem to hate me," I said.

"Humans deal with other people usually for what they can get out of them. You must go into other people's lives to give to them...

"Your sons and daughter, your two brothers and sisters hurt you because you want love, admiration, recognition from them. They have nothing to give. They can only take.

"Remember, you deal with them by words. Words are empty. I am talking to you by words, but I never do. In heaven the spirits meld one with the other by feelings and images. They know everything about you when you join them in heaven. Nothing can be hidden. You cannot do that with your family.

"With your family, you deal in words. Words hide whole worlds when people discourse. With a screen of words, your family – and you, yourself – let people know only what they want them to.

"You feel you owe your family something, you feel guilty. You owe then nothing, because in any person, however evil, there lies only a chance for something new, something better. Your family will ever be a chance for something better, however bitter you find them.

"What do you say?"

I had nothing to say. I was numbed.

At last, I spoke. "You said you could tell me many things."

Words appeared on the wall. When I read them, they vanished.

After half a minute, new words came up.

This went on and on. I had no sense of time.

Once, a voice told me to change the film in the camera.

I don't know whether hours passed.

The words stopped.

I called out into the empty cave, "Are You there! Are You there!"

The air was silent.

Heavily, slowly, I set up the table, with my word processor, and transcribed till dusk.

Next morning, after breakfast, I went on transcribing.

And this is what I wrote.

Slaughter and utter destruction fills the Bible, human history. Whole cities put to the sword.

Most men are killers, at their lowest level. Their way out is mindless violence, to kill the other.

You are the same with your rifle.

To kill yourself, because 'yourself', your body and your mind are 'other' to you.

"Your others inside you make you suffer... agonize.

Often your agony becomes unbearable.

You live on earth. Earth orbits in the cosmos, and your cosmos is one of many dimensions which are invisible to you. All these are parts of My Whole – trillions upon infinite trillions of parts do I have.

You are God's equal. You are My equal, in all my glory. No evil can harm your Spirit – your only harm comes from your human mind and how it registers pain.

Without pain, you would use your forefinger to stir sugar into your boiling coffee.

That is why I gave you pain.

The world of your Spirit is real. Your human mind, with its unreal words, lives in an unreal Universe, which is but a hologram, of My creating.

Your mind is not aware of your Spirit, but your Spirit knows your mind. Your mind stains your Spirit, and your Spirit carries all your mistakes and sufferings into heaven for all the Spirits to share, and to learn from.

For your mind, the way out, all too often, is mindless violence and killing.

Who are you? What is your personality? Why are you the way you are?

Your Spirit brings a highly individual personality to you, from eternity, and this stamps your mind.

Your mind builds up the rest of yourself, your ego.

On death, the mind dies and you suffer egocide.

Your ego dies, vanishes.

Your Spirit, perhaps with its personality added to, grown – or wounded and hatefully besmirched by a monster of a mind – goes back to its home in heaven, carrying memories of its life here, from which it and other Spirits learn.

Do not curse all that is evil in the world. Rather, say to yourself, "What have I done to change it?"

Western theologies say that I dictate what you must do.

I have created you with free will – I have said, "Let there be free will on earth as there is in heaven."

Your Spirit has incarnated in your body to live a new awareness, a level of awareness not possible in heaven. Even your groans are a new form of awareness, an awareness shared by the Godhead and by Me.

Who lives a full life? Those few who live with love at every moment, in every chance of fortune. Your wife was one such – now she is a glorious Spirit whose light outshines many in heaven.

Don't live fearfully. Don't live with a fire hose in your hand, waiting for your home on earth to catch fire.

When you think to yourself, you have a stream of consciousness – not a stream of talk inside your head.

At lightning speed.

You use scraps of words, blurs of images and flashes of feelings. You don't need the entire word – just a fragment gives it to you.

Someone has called this thinking to yourself *mentalese.*

Your Spirit tries to join in – but it is usually drowned out by the onrush of your mind.

When you think – "I could have said this" – or "I'm going to say that" – you form complete sentences with words.

But your Spirit seldom uses words. For the enlightened, their stream of consciousness, their inner mental business, is not in *mentalese* but in *spiritualese.*

In their inner mental stream, the voice of their Spirit rules.

Ordinary people know this sometimes when they listen closely to religious music or to religious chants.

When a body, a mind and an incarnated Spirit become one, God becomes flesh, and heaven dwells upon a sliver of the earth.

I will enter into a covenant with you. I, the Holy Spirit, come out of the changeless Godhead into change and time, will give you always what you ask. On your part – you will ask Me.

If you want something for yourself, then I want that for you too. I don't say – I'll give you this, and will not grant you that. What you want, I want for you.

However foolish it is, your mistake will teach and guide you.

God created your indwelling Spirit in His Own image.

Do not think of Myself, the Eternal Spirit, or the Godhead, as some unimaginably distant and aloof deity. Think of Us as persons, of the same image as yourself.

Perfected Persons, but nonetheless, like yourself.

The glory of God is that you shall return to dust, and your incarnate Spirit shall go to God, for there is nowhere else for your Spirit to go.

Place no faith in the Scriptures, in the so-called Word of God. You must experience Me yourself – you and I together.

Your indwelling Spirit has ten thousand ways
of Beingness here on earth.

Some things in the Bible are true. The Bible says God created you in his own image – your incarnated Spirit is the true and very substance of God Himself.

To find yourself, you must find out what you are not. Not This. Not That.

You must discover I Am This.

Few people ever stop to think what they are NOT.

Do I know the future?

Yes.

Do you know?

No.

As I live within your mind, your thoughts and feelings, I cannot know the future – I can only know what you know.

God created your indwelling Spirit in the image and likeness of the Godhead.

It is not My job to make your life for you.

I can guide and help.

Love is the only truth. It is the all and the only and the one.

When you love, you are in touch with Me and with the Godhead in heaven.

God created your Spirit in love...for love...of love.

You are thinking, he who loves others today goes naked in a savage world. If you don't fight, today's world will wipe you out.

If you don't hold high-denomination banknotes of love, then don't be parsimonious with love's small change, its copper coins.

For those who are rude, sour, indifferent or threatening to you, you can be lavish with the small copper coins of pleasantness, of friendliness.

Or are you too weak?

Kindness to the old – often in pain – is a small coin to give.

People cling to their bodies, but I have made you so that in the later years, the pains of the body will fill most minds and leave room for little else.

In their pain, the old will curse their bodies, and turn away from this world in resignation and weariness.

Most will thirst for the compassion and love they ignored in the self-assured – or in the haughty – days of their strength.

Your Spirit tries to create, but your mind and body are usually unyielding. Your mind plots and plans and guesses. Your body lives through sensations and warning aches and pains.

You must learn to see yourself as a Spirit, see yourself as holy, before you can see others as deserving, lovable, blessed, unique – even though they only give you hostility, hate, rejection, as your own family in Melbourne does.

The world is a hologram which I have created.

But the world you see is another hologram of your own making.

You think that the protons and the neutrons stay in the nucleus of the atom because of the strong force. They stay there because I "painted" them there in my hologram. Each of you lives in his or her hologram; and weeps at how bitter is the imagined "reality".

Know that your life is not finding out about yourself, but creating an ever-new, richer hologram. The poorest in spirit live in a lacklustre, black and white hologram.

Everything you do is from fear or from foolish desire.

States of enlightened-being, over a long time, will lead to a full life for you on earth, and even to earthly success.

Watch for coincidences. You have seen many in your life.

There are no coincidences. When you string together the coincidences over the years, you will see they point along the road of your life. They are one of the ways I have tried to help you. Some are on watch for coincidences. Others are blind to them.

Although I have given you full freedom, God does have a plan – a wide, wide plan.

Wide as it is, you cannot go outside of it... you cannot do or think anything outside of God's plan.

Because you are part of God.

You can look about you and see the obligations you yourself and others impose on you.

Or you can look seeing them as new chances – you can look about you seeking new chances.

You have taken a very great chance coming to this far and lost corner of Australia.

I beckoned you, but you could have closed your eyes against Me.

I wished all my prophets to tell you not that "I am holier than thou,' but "You are as holy as I am."

Alas, my prophets have taught what suited them, not Me.

You ask, Who am I exactly, what is God really like?

The Godhead is changeless and unchanging, torrential, blazing love from everlasting to everlasting.

At the Will of the Godhead, I came forth to enter into change and time.

I created the Universes, each in its own Dimension.

The maelstrom of energy and light in a thousand million galaxies is but a shining drop of water beside My Might and My Majesty.

Modern Western man mocks me. But primitive man sensed I was out there, awed at my power.

I wrote the DNA code for the neurons that give a child at birth a full instinct for grammar, that he might talk. Mocking modern man cannot write that code.

I am He Who created the ribosome, the miracle that turns RNA into amino acids. I await mocking man to build a ribosome. To understand it!

Can I not then succour you who love Me, be an ever-present comfort in your brief sojourn on this earth?

I will help you always. You can always come to Me. If you rise higher and higher, it will be because you want to, not because I demand it, expect it of you.

I love you the same, forever, whatever you do or do not do.

I give My divine energy to all my human creation, so that you may seek your uncreated Spirit which has come to dwell in your earthly, earthy body.

Make a picture in your mind of a full life as you would want it to happen – keep dreaming that dream and I will make it come true.

Your indwelling Spirit yearns to grow in beauty and awareness. That is why it has incarnated in a human.

The triumphs of the mind and body in this world are of small matter to it.

I have given you free-will. Yet preachers and priests say that if you do not submit to God, you will go to Hell.

Is that the free-will I have given you?

Your Spirit loves unconditionally. It is your human quest to seek that love, to become conscious of your Spirit that dwells in you.

Why your suffering?
Because you are aware of the elation of victory, the despair of defeat. You're aware of hope, of joy, of loss, of fear.

No one finds peace in the storm.

Other people are hurting you. Rejection and hate.

Think on the glorious Spirit within you. Two million years ago, I placed the Spirit in hominids.

Why? So that you are not simple, perishable clay.

Now you are part of Me – part of the Godhead, bearer of life from everlasting to everlasting.

Your incarnated Spirit longs for that hour of glory when you become conscious of it, and, now Enlightened, you let it show you the way – when your mind becomes one with it.

You'd like to come to Me more often with your problems, but you're not sure I'll settle things for you. You don't doubt that I *can*... you do doubt whether I'll care to.

You have little faith.

In your sojourn on earth, you have two choices – you can make a living chasing that coloured paper, money; or you can make a life.

As a geologist travelling in deserts and mountains, you did the two things.

But making your living came first, and now you are come to this place with a rifle.

Most people believe God talks only to some chosen people. Most people believe that lets them out – or they don't believe in Me anyway.

Most people listen to what others tell them, if they listen at all.

God is not to be found only in religion, and on Sundays.

You find me everywhere, at every minute.

Religion tries to reveal me.

It fails badly.

Bless misery, affliction and ruin, because from these come growth towards the Spirit, your true Self.

Growth towards your Spirit is My hope for you.

Your Spirit incarnated in your body with the dream of rising to higher levels, to higher awareness and to higher love.

Some people in their lives do rise up, grow selfless to their earthly selves.

When the Spirit takes over, it abnegates the mind.

People call such people selfless.

Mother Teresa of Calcutta was one such person.

Are you here, today, a person who has become who you are, from what has happened to you, or from what you decided on throughout the days of your life?

You are here on earth to live fully, and to do that, you need know the heights of your incarnated Spirit and fix your life there.

Your days on earth are not days of discovery, but of becoming. I created you, that you might create yourself, from minute to minute, hour to hour – create a human who seeks the spiritual path.

You learn unknowingly. Each day, you need show only what you have learned so far.

You build a wall brick by each brick.

You cannot lay the next course up in the air.

How puny is the human mind. You build wondrous machines, but they crash.

Your wise men say – you came from slime, gases, sunlight and lightning.

Every minute, a hundred thousand things happen in your sixty million million million cells inside you.

You have 100,000 proteins which toil away within you, many often thousands of amino acids long dictated by My DNA code. They have to fold up, to fit one with the other, like a key and lock. Each has its "sports coach" to show it how to fold. A wrong amino acid can stop them.

Your wise men wonder — which came first, the protein or its "coach"? I made them at the same instant. The "coaches", without their proteins, had no reason to be.

Without their "coaches" to coach them, the proteins were immobile.

Some slime, some gases, some lightning!

What human wisdom!

Joy it is to know you are undying, deathless, immortal. The millions who have nearly died, gone to heaven and come back into their bodies know it.

Envious, proud and wise men say it was a trick of the brain.

Some brain! Some wisdom!

Bliss it is for those who have found union with their Spirit, found their own I AM, and finally know what it means to say I AM.

Your mind lives.

Your deathless, undying Spirit IS.

This is what I want from you.

That My Awareness be enriched through you.

Your body and your mind are one, but I have split them off from your Spirit. The highly spiritual, enlightened ones live in their Spirit with the Holy Substance, the Divine Sum of All, Myself.

Nothing in the life you live is real, save your life in Me.

What is real is not My hologram but your Spirit that inhabits your body and mind.

You are a geologist who has worked much of your life in the Australian outback. This is your affirmation of your life in this stay of yours on earth.

Yet what you do is holy because it defines who you are in your life on this level, affirms you before Me.

I have created you so that your deepest need, your deepest yearning is to love and be loved – recover that love you had in heaven before your birth.

All humanity conspires to frustrate it.

What is it like when you come closer to being enlightened?

Not the decisions of your mind but the choice of your Spirit guides what your body does, and what your mind thinks.

Do you do things to make yourself happy? Or are you happy – and you act out of happiness? Blessed are those who live like that.

Every single thought, every feeling, every prayer to Me, everything you say – is a creation, and reflects in God's Awareness.

Keep not your eyes staring at your feet, but lift up your gaze to horizons, to the starry heavens.

Within yourself, seek the depths, seek your unseen Spirit.

Your Spirit has ten thousand ways of being here on earth.

Your mind has very few ways on how to live out your life.

Your Spirit never becomes attached to this world. Your Spirit cleaves ever to Me and to the Godhead.

The Spirit is centred upon you, but its first love is God.

On your death, it rises readily from your body. Looking down at your inert form, often it does not recognise you, the body from which it has just departed.

Western theologians – priests and preachers – speak of a God of ire, a jealous God, a stern God who judges and damns.

This is some distorted deity from unhappy minds.

You believe that God says "yes" to some prayers and "nay" to others, or if not "no", He says "later on". God hears all your prayers, but the Godhead does not intervene in the cosmos.

I do.

But what can I do?

I answer the prayers I can – other prayers I cannot, because what you ask is locked into nature's laws, or into the ineludible circumstances of other people's lives.

You can never go astray.

Heaven is your home, is the end of every life's journey.

Heaven is infinite...you can't miss it, however badly you aim.

The love in your mind for other people's minds, and perhaps for their bodies – make it not a clinging love.

Let them come and go freely. Don't try to bind them with their dependence – afterwards, they cannot manage on their own.

Who are you really?

You are your Spirit.

This is the greatest thing humanity faces... to pass from the mind, which dies when the brain dies, to being conscious of the indwelling, personal Spirit.

To heed it.

Your Spirit never imposes itself.

It pleads, it nudges, it hopes...

Your mission is to live your life fully – to the full – and to help others to do the same.

If you do not live your life to the full, you are empty. You won't fill the emptiness buying possessions – often he or she who has great possessions is the poorest, the most pitied in heaven.
Those with great possessions are those who clutch them most, share them least...

When you are enlightened, you can bear things that today you would call unbearable, intolerable.

When you see where you are at here on earth, and where you are going – to heaven – that is the beginning of wisdom.

You live in a world where societies are full of fear, where leaders fan those fears, and talk of terror.

Societies who believe in fear and terror, invite and attract calamity after tragic calamity.

I am the Holy Spirit, the Eternal Spirit – in ancient times they called me the Paraclete, from the Greeks; called me the Holy Ghost, The Divine Spirit come forth out of the Perfect Love and Infinite Awareness in heaven, God from God; they called me the Right-Hand of God, the Comforter, the Teacher sent among the men who I had created to help and give understanding.

These were some of My Names.

You may deny Christ, Buddha, Krishna, the Path of the Tao.

You cannot deny you have your Spirit incarnated in you, however much you may rage and shout that you have not.

Your Spirit --is in you.

You live on the earth. Earth orbits in the cosmos; its galaxy orbits galaxies that orbit galaxies. Your cosmos is one of many Dimensions which are now invisible to you.

All these are parts of my Whole – billions upon infinite billions of parts do I have.

You mould your own world, your own hologram of the world. You can see no other life than the one you create in your mind.

If you don't believe in God – and you always said you didn't – you cannot believe in the Perfect Being's ineffable and limitless love.

The ineluctable Being in heaven of infinite Awareness.

Men resist My call, resist their indwelling Spirit. The more they resist, the more they show they are resisting something that is really there.

When you create yourself, great are your rewards.

For Me, every person is golden, every one of their moments a joy or a sadness.

Grow in joy, at My side.

When your mountain of problems grows truly high, remember that if you found all the answers and had no problems left, your earthly life would come to a halt.

I will never leave you – I can't, for I made you. You are of Myself, of the Holy Spirit in this world, and you are of the ineffable Love and Awareness of the Godhead in heaven, of the blissful Being in the unchanging Now.

I have never said, "right" or "wrong", "do" or "don 't". That would take away from you that treasure, your priceless free will.

Because you have free will on earth as you do in heaven.

You do not come into this world trailing clouds of glory. Your mind is a blank. I have shaped you so that you cannot remember the outpouring of God's love, how God loved you beyond measure.

You live in this world to discover lovelessness, that you might yearn for the love you have lost.

Your life is not about getting somewhere.

You have already got somewhere – friends give you respect and envy, and what have you found, now you are where you are?

Even before you ask, I have heard you.

Do not implore Me, but thank Me without even asking first.

Always tell yourself – your life will change and change in this world, and then you will die.

You may now go on to live a new life – or you may die this afternoon at 5.15, when you are hurrying to an appointment at 6 pm.

Your life as it is today will not last.

I am in all. My divine purpose, My divine Will is in everything. My divine presence is in every grain of sand, is ever at your side.

Your vision is blurred. You're not sure of anything. The universe is but your confused hologram.
You wrack your thoughts, wrench your mind, but you still get your same hologram. Call upon Me, the Lord, your God of Love.

Lust not after the success of another, nor pity his failure, for your Spirit incarnate is reckoning your own success and failure.

I send my messages to all the inhabited planets, and have throughout millions of years.

I will send them, and send them again, to galaxies remote from you here on earth.

I will never stop sending them, and pouring out My love.

I, the Holy Spirit, will never force My will upon your Spirit. It is impossible for Me to do that.

Beware. You attract to yourself what you fear and what you desire foolishly.

Do not keep on saying, "This is bad", "This is not right." Don't judge, but instead, feel blessed when you decide for or against a step, for this is to live your life, to go forward. Bless yourself when what you decided, perhaps half-blindly, leads you upwards.

When you can't make up your mind, you worry. Don't.

Not to be able to make up your mind is a decision in itself – very often, the right decision.

I Am The Lord, your Very God. Through you, when you create and recreate yourself every minute, I am recreating Myself – with you and in you – as I have done in the whole of my created Universes, each one to its Dimension.

When you bless everyone, forgive everyone, look upon even a beggar with awe, you are praising Me and My creation.

Today, hundreds of millions in the West are pagans, and go uncomforted to the tomb.

They cling in despair to their bodily life, to their consciousness which they think death will extinguish.

When you worry, ask yourself one question.

What am I going to do about it?

Repeat those words a thousand times.

What am I going to do about it?

When you no longer care for possessions, but take the ascetic path, the paradox is that you will never lack for anything you need. You will become a rich man in your inner world, but the outer world will care for you as never before.

Because I am there.

Everything you do, everything you think, comes from foolish desire or from fear.

You can only go beyond that by love – each step into Love is a step towards enlightenment.

You don't believe your prayers to Me or to the Godhead will come true, often because you feel that what you are asking for is too good to be true.

What are the heights of human life, a sublimely full life?

A life of joyful love.

My messages come in a multitude of ways over millions of years.

Try to listen.

Your experience is always the wisdom of hindsight. You strike into the unknown, always blind in your trial and error.

I have humbled you thus – to have to live by trial and error.

Ask yourself, "Do I wish to know my indwelling Spirit in its fullness, or do I wish to find one part of it, to begin with?"

Sometimes it is better to take small steps to get to a place so hidden.

Should you overcome your foolish desires? I say to you, desire the full life, the life of love.

It is better to fulfil the desires of the needy than to satisfy empty, foolish ones of your own.

When you get together with another person, you try to window-dress one part of yourself or another.

The other person always disappoints you.

Then you try to take over one part or another of the other person.

More disappointment.

Most of humanity is at loggerheads.

There is one answer alone to human existence.

Love.

All else is suffering, deprivation, fear and foolish desires.

Think of each experience, however hateful, as a hidden gift which you can respond to in a hundred creative ways.

You have not come to earth on trial, and although almost everyone fails anyway, yet you do not need to be "saved".

Hell is believing that you need to be "saved".

Your fears and foolish desires keep you from fullness in your life.

Fullness is joy and love.

The enlightened live with love every second of the day, in every mischance.

Your wife was like that.

Hear what I say. Heaven and earth may pass away, but your Spirit shall live, and has already lived, from everlasting to everlasting.

Your Spirit incarnates in your body with the dream of rising to higher levels, to higher awareness and to higher love.

Some people do rise up.

In this world, you own nothing. You are on the brief crossing of a bridge to heaven.

In your fullness, you can give and give.

Despite the preachers and the priests, you have nothing you are obliged to fulfil, no exhortations you must answer to.

I send each of you here with a mission, but expect nothing and do not judge you.

I know you have come to this cave weary unto death.

But when you come close to Me, your despair and exhaustion disappear.

In the safety of My eternal Presence, you live anew.

With your rifle you want to abandon your journey.

You have been on this journey for an eternity before you were born.

You will go on with it for life everlasting after you fire that shot – or after you die at your appointed time.

You must eschew fear and foolish desire.

Perfect love casts out fear.

You have nothing to fear but your fears and
your foolishness.

Judge not nor condemn, because you can never know what really happened to that human being.

You have only to ask Me. Can you reach Me?

You will see how I come to you.

When you think you are right about life, talk to Me, and ask Me what I think.

What your body does is a reflection of your mental state.

Do not depend on your body acting to achieve a higher state of being – it satisfies only itself.

I have given you life on earth as a venture into the unknown.

Most people would like me to write the play first, so that they would know their parts before they step onto their life's stage.

I know what is going to happen, but I enter into you and share your blindness, your groping through the days of your life, that you may live to the full and not act an empty part, a part not of your making.

I have created you in My image, so that you can never live in fullness through your body and mind alone.

You are a holy trinity.

Your body is physical, your mind is non-physical and mental, and your Spirit is metaphysical.

Strive that this does not become an unholy trinity.

You often ask God for help, but deep within yourself you don't trust your own prayers.

Try thanking Me or the Godhead in advance – when you do that, you will be surer that what you want is really there and that you're going to get it.

To come close to someone does not mean that the other might complement or complete you.

You should fill their shortcomings, shore them up, be strong where they are weak, let them bleed out their sufferings in angry, vicious spates of words.

You should listen to them when no one else does.

When you pray, part of you wonders, will I answer you? Will I give you what you want?

You don't need to ask me anything. All that you may receive, I am ready to lavish it upon you.

Some teach of your karma, of debts you must pay by one reincarnation after another, often painful reincarnations.

Know that this is nothing more than the products of human imagination.

You can reincarnate if you want to – and some do, sometimes several members of a family together, to be joined in another life on a planet.

The world today horrifies you. It is the way it is because of ignorance, fear and foolish desires – often foolish desires in foolish leaders.

If you let me, I will lead you to places where you may grow and live more fully.

I can lead you to these paths, beside still waters – it is you who must walk forward, scale the heights, sit and meditate at the places I show you.

If you would do or have something, do not pine after it.

Act now. Decide to struggle along that path, to see whether it is a good path.

All your life you have thought you were your body – and when not your body, your mind.

When you die you will discover who you really are – your indwelling Spirit, which will carry the memory into heaven of what your mind has thought and your body done,

You have money and property. You could turn your back on your geology, sleep on your air mattress, and give yourself over to contemplation, meditation and communion with Me.

But you cannot even think of this till you enter in some sort of communion with your own Spirit.

The fear and desire in your mind are the opposite of everything your Spirit is.

Your Spirit is eternal.

Your immortal spirit dwells within your fragile dust.

Dust goes to dust, Spirit to the Light Everlasting.

You have come to this remote gorge laden with self-blame.

Stop blaming yourself.

Look at what you have decided to do and not to do. Seek out your decisions which were good ones, and dismiss those that were not.

While you would love your family, you do not have to do what they want you to, because evil often moves them.

I am always here when you call on Me. You see I am with you now, in this cave.

You must ask the questions and find the answers by trial and error, but I will always help and show you when you do not succeed.

Lovingly, I let each person walk his path through this world.

I never judge.

Your life is one of unending choices. You make them as best you can, by trial and error.

Do not castigate yourself when with the wisdom of hindsight you see you were wrong.

In your human ignorance, you make many mistakes, but you are often right too.

To err is human.

Forgive your own errors.

I will help you get what you want, if it is allowed to you.

I will help you do what you want to do.

I will help you go where you want to.

I will help you be what you want to be.

This way, you will learn wisdom – from your good choices and from your bad.

Sometimes you are confused.

Who am I? Why am I doing what I am doing? Am I going anywhere?

You have lost faith, and come here with a rifle.

Look at who you are not, at what you have not done.

That tells you very much about yourself too.

Have you ever thought that every day you could bless yourself and those around you?

I have created you most wondrously. You have billions of cells that are microscopic, yet inside them hundreds of thousands of things happen.

A cosmic expense of energy just to keep you on your feet and to give one smile.

You are here because your family tries to make you feel guilty – and guilty you feel.

Preachers and priests speaking in My name do this too.

Your Spirit has incarnated in your body to live a new awareness, a level of awareness not possible in heaven. Even your groans are a new form of awareness, an awareness shared by the Perfect Love in heaven and by Myself.

The life of most people on earth is to do things with their bodies, with their hands.

That is not My Plan.

Only through the incarnated Spirit can true changes come, but for most of humanity, their Spirit is invisible; many do not believe it is there.

I have given you full freedom.

Preachers and priests call this religious anarchy.

I give you My promise that in this freedom you can seek the full life – and only in this freedom.

I will do all that you need, but will do nothing that you won't do yourself.

I help you by helping you to help yourself.

Your life is an unending chain of decisions – so it is you who must decide to go upwards – stop where you are – or descend.

You came with life from the Godhead, from your Very God.

Filled with Being.

There is nothing else beside life – nothing more holy. The ineffable Treasure. The gift of the Perfect Love of the Godhead to all creation – to all heaven, to all the Universes.

Life pours forth unceasingly from the Godhead, the Divine Energy, inextinguishable and forever.

I have channelled this flow of life from the Godhead into your universe; and your scientists call it Zero Point Energy, or Dark Energy.

Your scientists measure this life flowing from the Godhead into your universe, as a force of a trillion trillion trillion trillion trillion trillion of trillions of tons per cubic centimetre, and say that this Zero Point Energy is chaotic; say it enters and exits your universe unendingly.

This Zero Point Energy – or Dark Energy – holds consciousness and awareness; it works with Me in the worlds and in your bodies.

Know that I am your Very God.

In heaven, all the Spirits form a divine oneness – they share all their feelings and images. The Godhead infuses them with love and bliss and glory.

You have always been part of this divine Oneness – for aeons upon aeons before you were born, and forever after you die.

Never forget you are a brief visitor in this body and in your human mind.

You think your life is about being busy, about money.   How little you understand. Your eternal, indwelling Spirit does not care a fig about how you earn your living. When you die, you will suffer egocide – much of your ego will die with the death of your mind.

Your Spirit cares only about your level of awareness, and how much of your ego will reach heaven, will be kept.

Your Spirit ever seeks perfect love, most high of the feelings, in heaven as here on earth.

Your body and mind DO.

Your Spirit IS, for everlasting.

I have created humanity in my own likeness, but bow rare are the souls who find their own Spirit, the Spirit who makes them Godlike, and not creatures of mere molecules.

If you choose growth towards your inner Spirit, you must partly turn your back on the world, on your mind and on your body.

Your Spirit is in a state of Being.

Your mind and body are in a state of doing.

The woe of most people is that their Spirit is a hapless watcher.

For Me, you are the most resplendent, the rarest and most prodigious life the Godhead has brought into being – each human is this in My eyes.

You have unhappy relationships with your brothers and sisters, and your children.

You must first love yourself.

Your wife loved everybody. She adored you, because she adored herself without even knowing she did.

You cannot do that. But you can at least try to love yourself knowingly.

If you must obey Me, as the priests and preachers say, then I have created nothing.

My joy, My love, My bearing you up, is for nothing.

Many people love Me, and bravely they tell the world.

Brave they are.

Most people will accept anything but this – a man who says he loves Me.

You cannot know Me until you stop telling yourself that I don't exist.

You cannot hear me while you say you are but Godless clay.

Your Spirit is all-knowing.

Nothing is hidden from it.

But it partakes in the ignorance, the suffering and struggles of your mind. Your Spirit ever seeks new sorts of awareness from you.

They tell you, think before you act.

Sometimes it is better to act before you think.

Love does that.

At times, consult your feelings, not your logic, before you act.

Everything that happens is to help your Spirit to grow to new levels outside of heaven.

Do you let your Spirit grow, or do you shut yourself down?

When you feel most forsaken, most cast
aside, most bereft, abject, despairing – then I
am closer to you than your own self.

You don't know yourself, but you think you do.

Your true nature is to be wholly loving, but you have never tried to live that way.

People who are spiritually enlightened live by loving.

God can feel no pain, but He suffers from
your pain.

You could not feel yourself your wife's pain,
but how you suffered for her!

Don't ever think you have to struggle for your own salvation. Salvation means saving yourself from Hell and its devils.

There are no devils, and Hell is a figment of the human mind. Preachers and priests use it to control their frightened congregations.

Your salvation is in your enlightenment, the realisation of your Spirit and its awareness, your true Self.

Ask me anything you like. Know that when you ask, if you can have it, I have already answered, long ago, over and over.

Who lives a full life? Those few who live with love in every moment, in every chance of fortune.

Your wife was one such — now she is a glorious Spirit whose Light outshines many in heaven.

You are fearful in this world because you ache after results, after success, after getting your way, getting what you want.

The end of any affair obsesses you – you want only an end that you desire.

Fear and foolish desire draws you in, makes you crouch, flee, cower, embrace your possessions with desperation.

Love opens you up, throws wide your arms, makes you welcome others, makes you smile, and share, and give, and raise your eyes up higher and higher...

What are your intentions?

Life flows from your intentions.

Too many people give up, give up on having intentions, and on hoping.

The things which most you fear will come to you often in the darkest hours.

Do not attract your fears to yourself.

Close your mind to them. I will send you answers.

With other people, expect nothing. When you do, you have a stricken affinity.

When you choose love, you will rise above the mere keeping of your body, rise above the need for the respect and envy of others.

You will rise towards your I AM, the quintessence of your Being, the projection of your Spirit into this world, into your mind.

Never forget. Everything passes away. Everything vanishes.

In your deepest despair, remember that too – everything – passes.

If God is not going to call you to your home in heaven at 3.10 pm, tomorrow is always a new day.

One reason for My creating you was for Me and the Godhead to experience, through your Spirit, non-love. That is possible only in this world.

You're angry at me for the agony of your wife's cancer.

Primitive man could not read or write, and suffered only 1/20 the pain that modern educated city people can feel.

Do not blame Me for today's industry, which pollutes and spawns cancer. Foolish mankind packs his cities with cars – noxious metal boxes. With today's wealth, the foolish gorge on meats, fats and sugars. As you eat and breathe, so do you reap and die.

A cruel toxic industrial chemical triggered your wife's long agony.

Now in heaven, she is a blinding light of bliss.

In heaven, we want the spirits to turn their backs on the earth, to forget.

Your wife refuses. She thinks of you, and for half her time, she returns to earth to your side.

She is standing beside you now, engulfing your body in her light, and your Spirit and hers are rejoicing together.

All is vanity.

On this planet, all your posturings, all your triumphs will go down into dust. All your failures and miseries – they will vanish without memory.

All My worlds, in all My universes, in all My Dimensions – invisible to you – will all perish and be forgotten.

I shape the forms first simply, then more fully, without haste. All live their epoch, and depart forever, as if they never were.

The fleetest feet freeze into rocky fossils.

Those with indwelling Spirits – their Spirits shall mount up to life everlasting.

All else will pass away, save the one imperishable reality – love. All love is caught up in the Godhead, forever.

On planets where the mind fully knows the indwelling Spirit – those beings live in Reality, in love.

Your love for your wife, and her love for you, already blazes in heaven.

If you cannot be loving, try to give disinterested care, charity; be open of heart and rich in your giving. Do not sully your eternal Spirit, closing in on yourself or hating.

If you cannot be loving, try to be pleasant, kind, hearty and of good cheer, cordial with those you don't like. Heaven will see you as more powerful. Fear to sully your Spirit.

If you cannot be loving, try at least to be benevolent, humane, benign with others – clement, accommodating with people you can't stand, compassionate. Greatly fear to sully your eternal Spirit; that the Spirits in heaven look upon your eternal Spirit with pity.

If you cannot be loving, at least be brotherly or sisterly, be generous, complaisant, try always to show the nobility of your Spirit in talking to others; talk to them with honour, force yourself to be obliging to those you detest. Sully never your eternal Spirit.

If you cannot be loving, be friendly, not harsh; be gentle and good-natured to all, be sympathetic to others, tender; be considerate to those who show you none. Fear ever to sully your eternal Spirit!

If you cannot be loving, try then to be affectionate, indulgent and not grasping; devoted, or fond of your fellows; be always forbearing and warm-hearted, a giver of bounty. Many a powerful or rich man has gone to heaven where his eternal Spirit has appalled the loving Spirits there.

If you cannot be loving, be mild, because the mild are powerful in the eyes of God, and they reign in heaven.

Some warn you that to come close to Me, to the Perfect Love of the Godhead, you must abjure earthly passions.

In themselves, those passions do not affect God. He simply loves the awareness of all that is you.

God works in mysterious ways. The bill you cannot pay, the cancer that kills a spouse, the job you lose, the house that is repossessed... My hand is in it all.

I will never try you more than you can bear, but am ever showing you the roads to saintliness, to higher being.

It might take you twenty or thirty years to understand something I have done.

Do you think your own thoughts, or those which others tell you to think?

Do you colour your own thoughts – or have your sons, your daughter, your brothers and your sisters coloured them?

Do you think thoughts for a full life, or do you think negatively, think of your rifle?

If you want an outside view of your life, look at what your body does and where it goes all day long.

Your body constrains your mind, unless you are enlightened.

When you suffer, you blame what has happened on this...or that...or on those people who have hurt you.

What happens...happens. Suffering is how you see it in your mind. Suffering is when you see your hologram twisted, wrenched...

Your hologram is not you...is not real.

Never dismiss a coincidence.

Nothing "just happens".

Remember I am taking part, am with you.

What is your want is My want.

What is your cry is My cry.

This is My love for you all.

I am a God of understanding and mercy.

I am the God of light and joy and goodness.

I am the God of patience and pardon, a comforter in your pain and an ever-present strength in your need...your guide in life's maze.

You cannot lie to your Spirit. You can lie to your mind that lives in your clay.

It is not enough to say, "I want to love." You must show love.

To be understanding of others, you must listen and accept their mental world.

Although you don't respect the way their minds work, you must make yourself feel respect, and move away from where you are standing.

Everything the preachers and priests tell you of your life after death – ignore it.

Western theologies are an artifice of the human mind.

You asked about My cruelty in creating hunting dinosaurs.

Had I created grazing dinosaurs only, over thousands of years, they would have numbered billions, and left not a scrap of vegetation on the face of the earth. Raptors, Tyrannosaurus Rex, and such hunting dinosaurs kept the numbers lower.

When a lion grabs an animal in its jaws, I have made the prey feel a total peace and resignation.

Are you the final glory of My design?

Your cities and machines rule the entire earth, your planet.

On other planets abide beings of My making who surpass you, some immeasurably.

Be humble.

You are as a ramshackle wayside inn on a far, far road.

When a place like Yellowstone explodes cataclysmically, you may vanish, and every last one of you will return to your heavenly home.

It will be as I dispose, when that day comes.

In a divine transport of creation, I Will into life billions upon billions of forms of my design in all My universes and Dimensions – forms that come, and perish, almost all without an indwelling Spirit.

While they live, the Godhead and I live in them to share their world – yea, even the world and life, minute by minute, of an insect.

Your scientists believe that they are the glorious crown of creation. They believe they alone know the rigorous truths – that the rest of you are ignorant, that they are your gods.

They teach that I designed nothing – that the accidental bustle of molecules put creation together. Their clinching proof against other protesting scientists who say that is mathematically impossible is that if I existed, I would not have wasted 500 million years on lesser forms, but would have rushed to create *them* – 500 million years ago.

Record this on your camera –

GOD LAUGHED. GOD WEPT.

How full is your life?

Does it show who you are, and Who Am I?
As you come closer to Me, you will feel love,
joy, blessings – and thankfulness to be alive.

Don't think I haven't heard the weeping in your heart.

You can take up your rifle.

But I am your ever-present comfort, am always with you.

After I finished writing out all the messages, I collapsed on my air-mattress beside the pool for a couple of hours.

Then I went for a long walk, climbing down the gorge, out into the country around, and got back at about sunset.

That night, I slept heavily in my mosquito tent inside the cave. Thunder and lightning woke me up once, and I heard heavy rain.

Next day was cloudless.

At midmorning, I went back into the cave, into its silence, its stillness.

I cried out. "Are You there? What must I do?"

Silent emptiness.

I called out again.

Two shining words came on to the wall.

"Go South".

The words faded.

Go south!

South where!

There was nothing down south!

To Broome, Dampier, Geraldton or Perth? Or take the inland road?

It was crazy.

Next morning, I packed up the Land Rover. I topped up my jerricans of drinking water to forty litres, and drove off slowly, on the tricky, bumpy two days of cross-country driving, to the far away surfaced road.

THE END